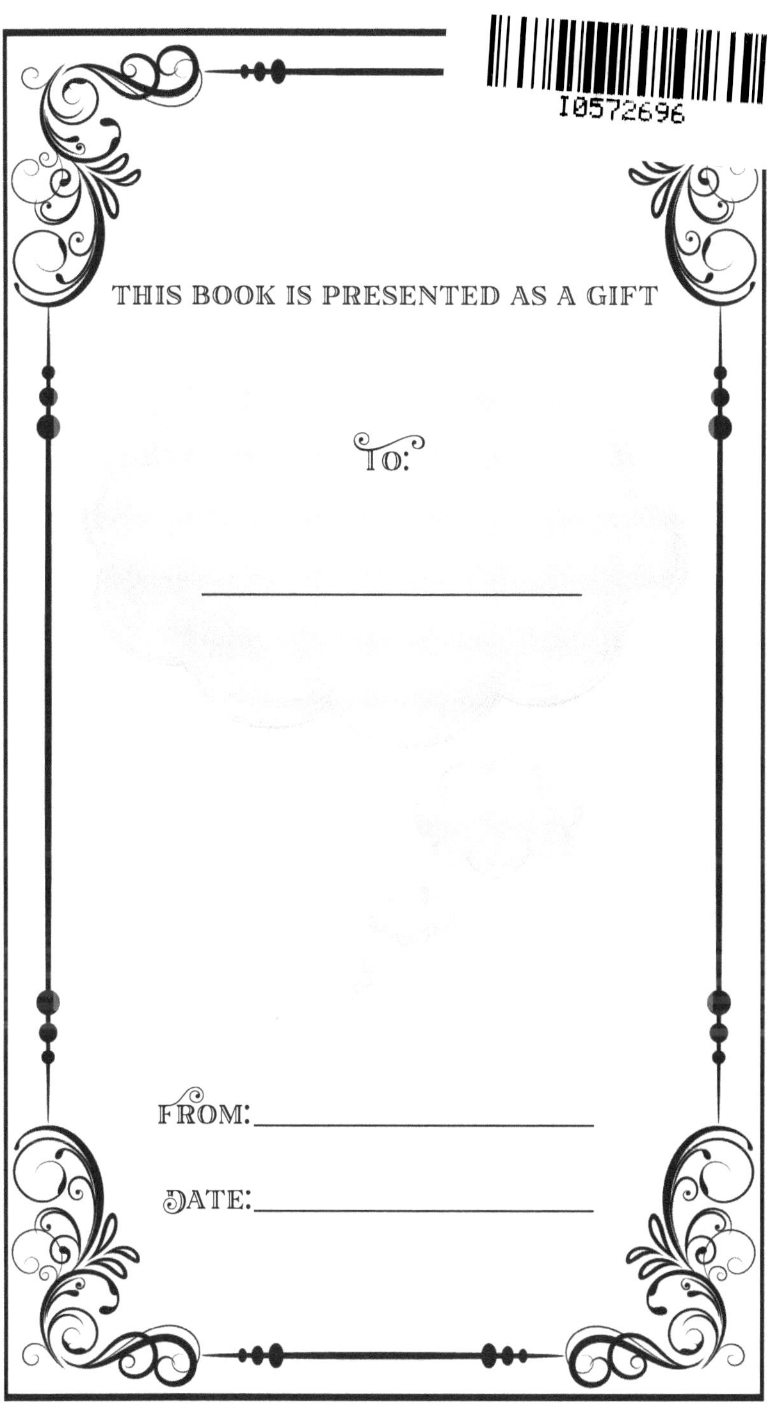

I0572696

Just an Idea
Copyright © 2024 by Yrana Rachele Avery

First Edition 2025

ISBN: 979-8-9919695-0-5 (hard cover keepsake edition)
ISBN: 979-8-9919695-5-0 (hard cover reader's edition)
ISBN: 979-8-9919695-3-6 (paperback reader's edition)
ISBN: 979-8-9919695-1-2 (paperback large edition)
ISBN: 979-8-9919695-2-9 (ebook)

Published by 987 More Ideas
www.987moreideas.com
publishing@987moreideas.com

Cover Design and Illustration by Yrana Rachele Avery
Edited by Melissa Stevens, Purple Ninja Editorial
Book Layout and Design by Dani Oliver, Yrana Rachele Avery
Back Cover Photo by Heaven Avery

Printed in the U.S.A

JUST AN IDEA

BOOK 1

An Inspirational, Feel-Good Story That'll Motivate You
to Stop Procrastinating and Get Your Bright Idea Off the Shelf!

a debut by

YRANA RACHELE AVERY

987
more ideas

publishing@987moreideas.com

To my husband, Sir Basil, who so bravely endured
the aftermath of my many sleepless nights while
writing and publishing this book.

To my three favorite knuckleheads, Heaven, Eden,
and Bishop, who so "willingly" served as my very
first readers, editors, critics, and captive audience.

And finally, to my mother, Michelle, my biggest
fan from whom I've inherited every ounce of my
obnoxiously vivid, slightly offbeat, and wildly
overactive imagination.

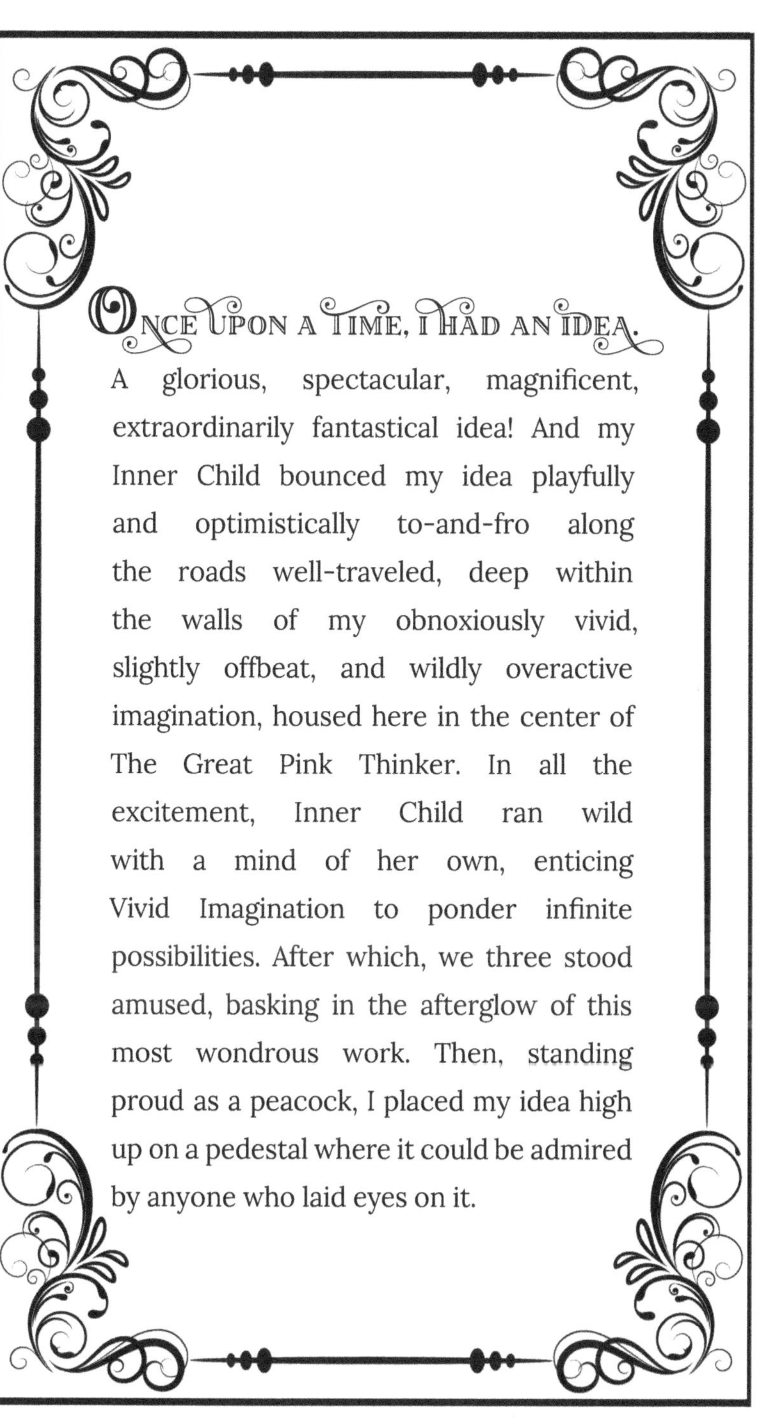

Once Upon a Time, I had an Idea. A glorious, spectacular, magnificent, extraordinarily fantastical idea! And my Inner Child bounced my idea playfully and optimistically to-and-fro along the roads well-traveled, deep within the walls of my obnoxiously vivid, slightly offbeat, and wildly overactive imagination, housed here in the center of The Great Pink Thinker. In all the excitement, Inner Child ran wild with a mind of her own, enticing Vivid Imagination to ponder infinite possibilities. After which, we three stood amused, basking in the afterglow of this most wondrous work. Then, standing proud as a peacock, I placed my idea high up on a pedestal where it could be admired by anyone who laid eyes on it.

And there it sat.
And sat.

And sat some more.

Because, after all, it was just an idea.

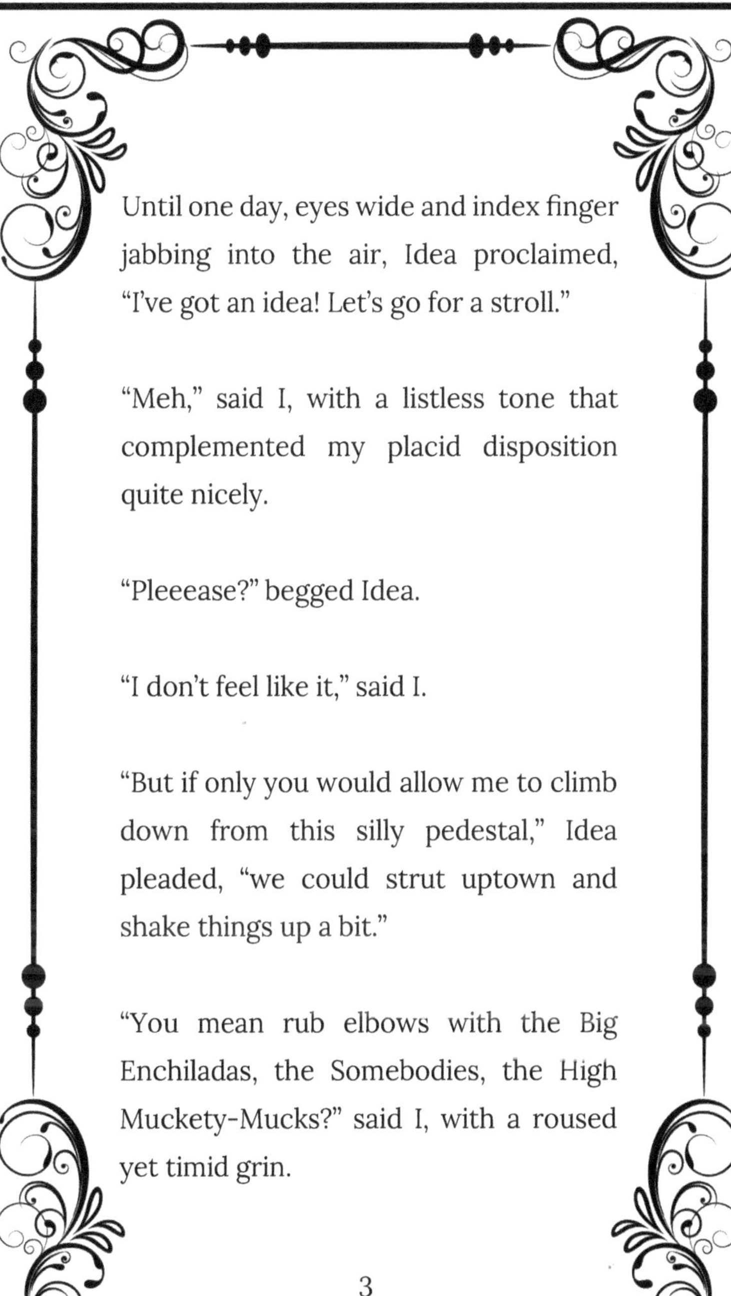

Until one day, eyes wide and index finger jabbing into the air, Idea proclaimed, "I've got an idea! Let's go for a stroll."

"Meh," said I, with a listless tone that complemented my placid disposition quite nicely.

"Pleeease?" begged Idea.

"I don't feel like it," said I.

"But if only you would allow me to climb down from this silly pedestal," Idea pleaded, "we could strut uptown and shake things up a bit."

"You mean rub elbows with the Big Enchiladas, the Somebodies, the High Muckety-Mucks?" said I, with a roused yet timid grin.

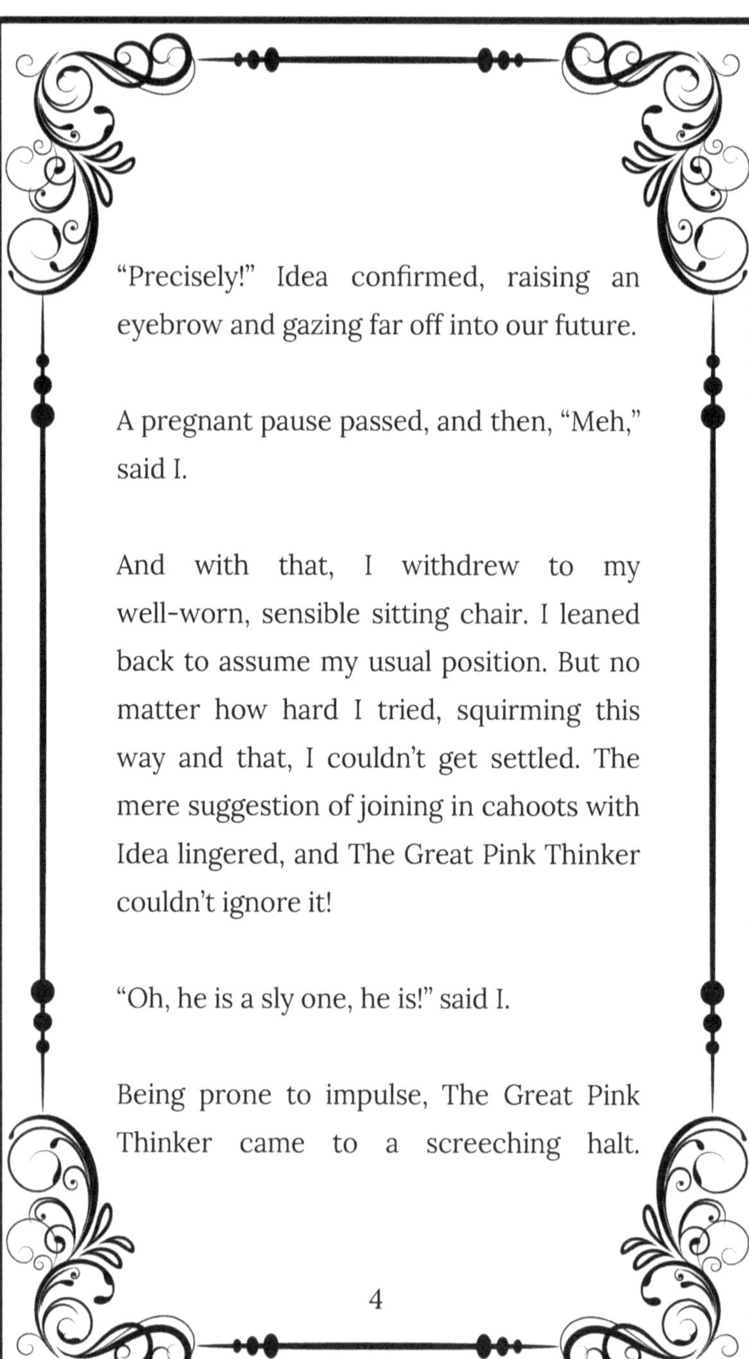

"Precisely!" Idea confirmed, raising an eyebrow and gazing far off into our future.

A pregnant pause passed, and then, "Meh," said I.

And with that, I withdrew to my well-worn, sensible sitting chair. I leaned back to assume my usual position. But no matter how hard I tried, squirming this way and that, I couldn't get settled. The mere suggestion of joining in cahoots with Idea lingered, and The Great Pink Thinker couldn't ignore it!

"Oh, he is a sly one, he is!" said I.

Being prone to impulse, The Great Pink Thinker came to a screeching halt.

Without thinking, it shifted gears and defaulted to perpetual ponder mode. Like clockwork, my foot began to tap an erratic solo on the living room floor while my fingertips drummed up a duet with the armrest. Rats! It was too late. Idea's idea caused a glitch that triggered a vicious cycle of meddling thoughts that plagued The Great Pink Thinker, and I found myself in a pickle.

Still determined to nip the urge to think about Idea, I clenched my fingers into a tight fist, but my wrist, intent on running its course, betrayed me and quickened the tempo. Refusing to be outdone, I turned my attention toward my foot—my hand's lowly sidekick—and pressed my sole hard against the floorboards. But my toes, lacking a mind of their own and powerless to resist, upheld the rhythm, and the band played on.

In a last-ditch effort to drown out the thought of Idea's idea—and the opening act that accompanied it—I resorted to the unthinkable. Without reservation, I welcomed back the catchy tune that had just last week been stuck inside my head, tormenting me for days on end. Yet despite all my determination, the thought, in a desperate move to avoid being cast into a sea of forgetfulness, hid deeper in the crevices, securing its place in my long-term memory. Finally, helpless against the power of suggestion, I gave in. I came to realize that simply thinking about a thing essentially required zero effort on my part. That being the case, and being a bit of a daydreamer anyway, for a time I did just that.

But after a while, again, I yearned for a place to kick up my feet. So I plucked Idea down from his royal throne and repurposed his pedestal into a nice, sturdy, comfy footstool and stuck Idea on a nearby shelf.

And again, there Idea sat.
And sat.
And sat some more.

Because, after all, it was just an Idea.

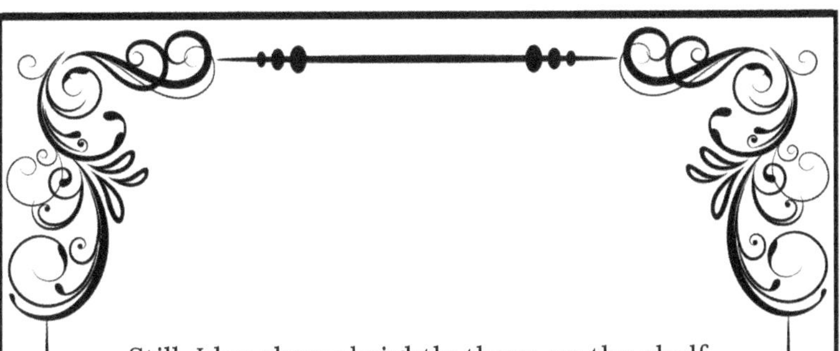

Still, Idea shone brightly there on the shelf among the riffraff. But because he was alive and well, and could think and move and be, Idea grew anxious in his present company.

"I was not created to sit upon a shelf!" Idea protested toward Knick Knack, who simply stared off into No-Place-In-Particular with a blank grimace on his face.

Knick Knack stood his ground, unashamed of his novelty-grade handiwork and unaware that his cheap ceramic potbelly bore a sizable crack just above his trousers. Well, this injustice made Idea even more anxious, and so Idea began to stir up quite a ruckus!

With an irritable pout and taunting me from the corner of his eye, Idea wedged his foot beneath an artificial plant and tipped it ever so gently, until it swirled about and teetered on its edge. Then, just as if he willed it to do so, the plant dominoed an old family photo, a few miscellaneous encyclopedias, and a basketful of trinkets before crashing to the ground! Pleased as pie and trying hard to appear inconspicuous, Idea stuffed his hands into his pockets and spun in the opposite direction, mimicking Knick Knack's fixed stare into No-Place-In-Particular.

"Hmmm, I see you're becoming a bit of a rabble-rouser over here, aren't you?" said I, suspiciously approaching the nearby shelf.

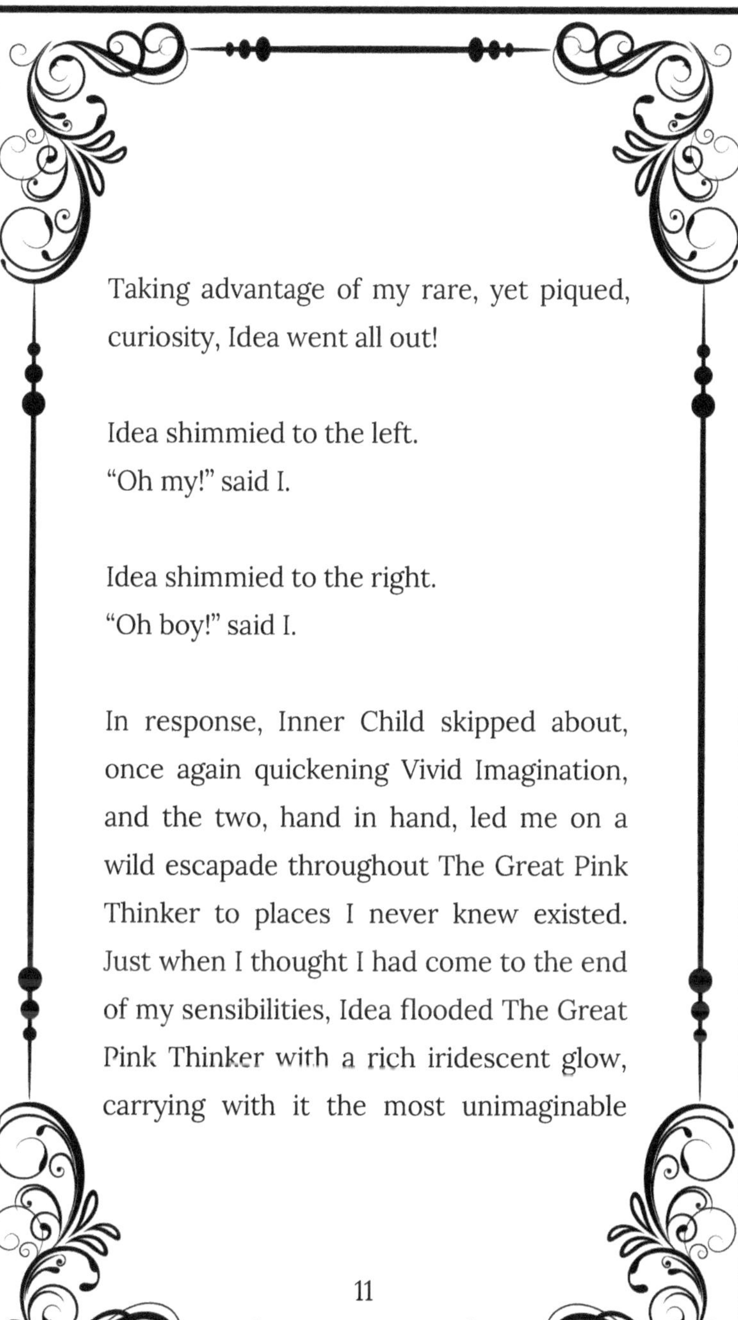

Taking advantage of my rare, yet piqued, curiosity, Idea went all out!

Idea shimmied to the left.
"Oh my!" said I.

Idea shimmied to the right.
"Oh boy!" said I.

In response, Inner Child skipped about, once again quickening Vivid Imagination, and the two, hand in hand, led me on a wild escapade throughout The Great Pink Thinker to places I never knew existed. Just when I thought I had come to the end of my sensibilities, Idea flooded The Great Pink Thinker with a rich iridescent glow, carrying with it the most unimaginable

dreams that persuaded me to believe
I could do anything!

"What a bright idea you are!" said I.

The Great Pink Thinker had never housed such glory and could scarcely contain such a wondrous work. It wasn't long before I was spending my days browsing books like *Bright Ideas and How to Grow Them* and *Ideas: The Good, The Bad, and The Downright Ridiculous*. I endured more than a few sleepless nights thumbing through titles like *Hey, What's the Big Idea?* and *That's a Great Idea You've Got There, Now What?* But the most valuable two cents that sprung me into action hailed from the bestseller Your Big Idea and How Not to Screw It Up!

I fed him. I groomed him. I showered him with adoration and daydreamed about introducing Idea to the four corners of the world.

For a while, I found myself entertaining Idea. I took him for a drive along the countryside, and when we stopped to smell the roses, Idea cut loose, and I found myself chasing him through fields of beauty in the midst of thorns. I broke out in a sweat and realized Idea was more work than I'd expected. I was pleasantly overjoyed, but the thought of keeping up with Idea eventually overwhelmed my soul.

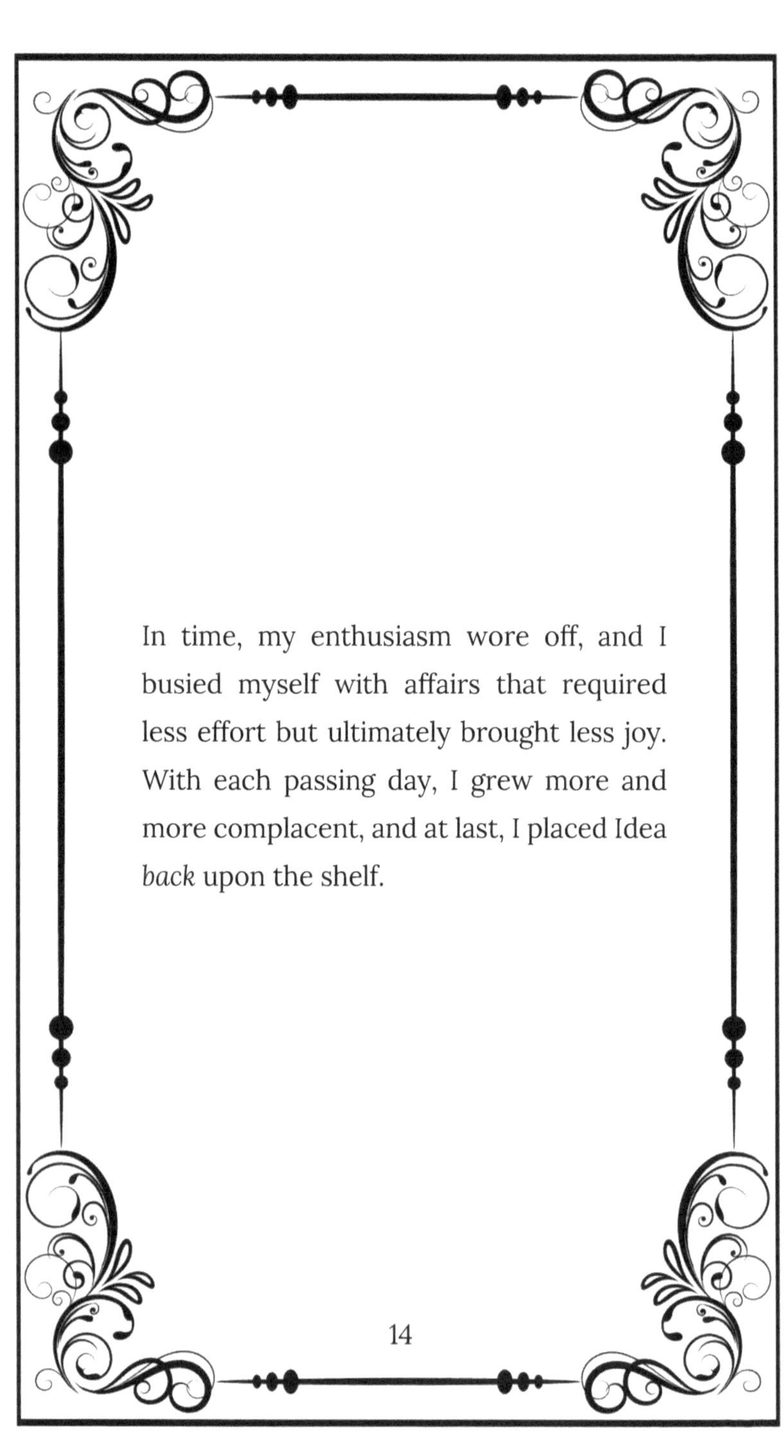

In time, my enthusiasm wore off, and I busied myself with affairs that required less effort but ultimately brought less joy. With each passing day, I grew more and more complacent, and at last, I placed Idea *back* upon the shelf.

Where again, he sat.

And sat.

And sat some more.

Because, after all, it was just an Idea.

Well, Idea did not like this one bit! Every time I sauntered past the shelf, Idea would flash visions of what could have been in my direction. But all I could ever muster up to say was *meh*.

After a good while, Idea's shenanigans became a bit of a nuisance to me, and in the end, I banished him to the furthermost corner of the tip-top tier of the shelf. From this unfortunate new point of view, Idea could now plainly see that the crack in his potbellied shelf-mate was actually quite extensive. The imperfection circled around Knick Knack's back to his plump rump, careening upward between his suspenders before settling at the edge of a ghastly chip on the very top of his cheap ceramic head. What a pity. Not even Knick Knack, who was still staring into oblivion, clueless to the damage he had sustained —no, not even Knick Knack—had suffered the likes of this height.

It was dark there.
It was cold there.
It was dusty there.

From far above, Idea realized he was no longer the center of my attention. Sadly, he took notice of me enjoying the simple pleasures of other people's bright ideas. Only those ideas were lucky enough to have been nurtured and then bound in a book, or produced on a screen, or sold in a store.

Idea sighed deeply.

And then sat.
And sat.

And sat some more.

Because, after all, it was just an Idea.

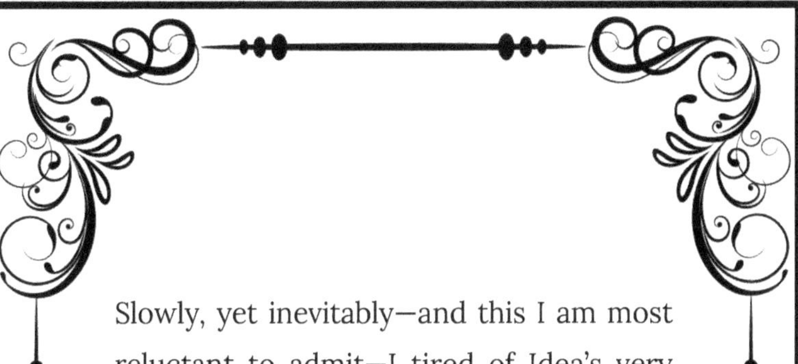

Slowly, yet inevitably—and this I am most reluctant to admit—I tired of Idea's very presence. Merely knowing of his existence, hovering there on the top shelf and lurking among the shadows, gave me much dread. So without hesitation, I yanked Idea from his hiding place, tossed him into my memory box, raced up the stairs into the attic, shoved the box straight away into my keepsake trunk, slammed the lid tight, clicked the padlock, and threw away the key!

"There!" said I. "That's that! Out of sight, out of mind!"

And there Idea remained, locked away in my keepsake trunk.

And then sat.
And sat.

And sat some more.

Because, after all, it was just an Idea.

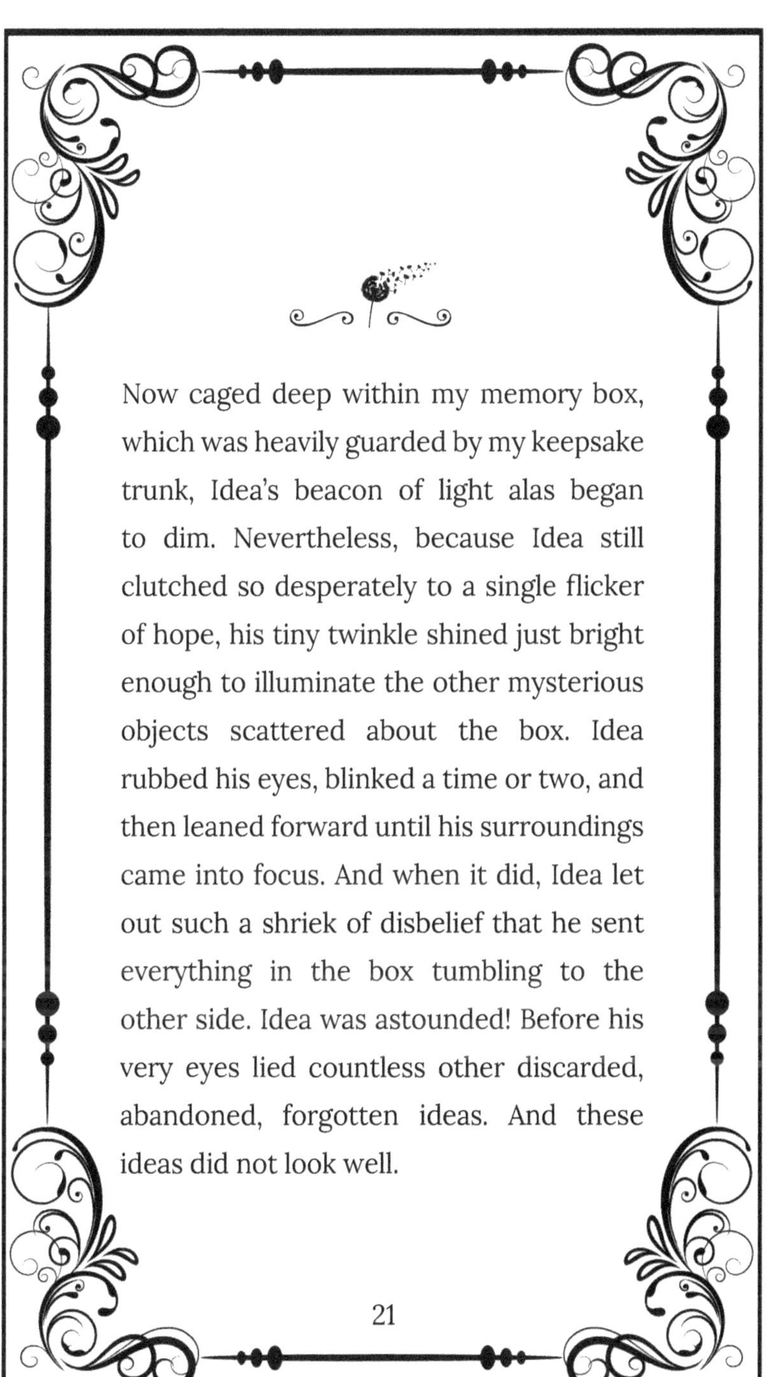

Now caged deep within my memory box, which was heavily guarded by my keepsake trunk, Idea's beacon of light alas began to dim. Nevertheless, because Idea still clutched so desperately to a single flicker of hope, his tiny twinkle shined just bright enough to illuminate the other mysterious objects scattered about the box. Idea rubbed his eyes, blinked a time or two, and then leaned forward until his surroundings came into focus. And when it did, Idea let out such a shriek of disbelief that he sent everything in the box tumbling to the other side. Idea was astounded! Before his very eyes lied countless other discarded, abandoned, forgotten ideas. And these ideas did not look well.

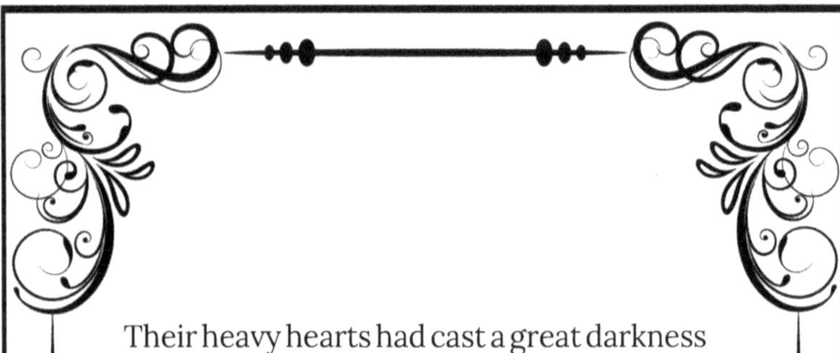

Their heavy hearts had cast a great darkness throughout the box, crushing their spirits and smothering their precious lights. Their once brilliant luster had tarnished to a dull, gloomy gray. Their radiant glow had diminished to a mere foggy mist. The poor Discarded Abandoned Forgotten Ideas now appeared so translucent that they had, in essence, faded into nothingness. Realizing his imminent fate, Idea lost all hope, and finally, inconsolable, let out a faint cry.

One by one, each idea joined in. And with each whimper added, their faint cries, all at once and without warning, swelled into one enormous, wailing bellow. Like a hot air balloon unhitched from its tether,

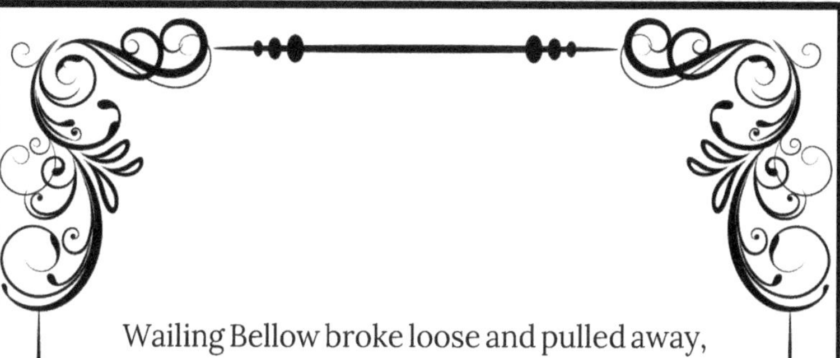

Wailing Bellow broke loose and pulled away, separating from his Discarded Abandoned Forgotten Ideas. Then incidentally, Wailing Bellow seeped out of the box, and against all odds, escaped the trunk!

Free at last, yet heartbroken to leave behind his Discarded Abandoned Forgotten Ideas—more truthfully his better halves —still caged deep within the memory box and heavily guarded by the keepsake trunk, Wailing Bellow looked back at his former dungeon and made a solemn promise to seek help for a much-needed rescue. Vowing to return, he quickly rose to the ceiling of the attic, eased between two loosened boards, then hoisted himself up and out onto the rooftop, where he was triumphantly swept into the outside world.

Now floating aimlessly about in the great outdoors, Wailing Bellow was caught up in a soft, quiet breeze that gently escorted him down the street, around the corner, and out of town.

Or at least that's how Vivid Imagination dutifully described it to me after I'd blatantly squandered my courtship with Idea. I, of course, was not there—not privy to witness Idea's new adventures—so my insight into this unexpected turn of events was left solely to her, Viv, my wild and overzealous and all too often, unpredictable Vivid Imagination. So, by all accounts in regard to Idea's whereabouts—whether fact or fantasy, truth or trumped-up—Viv's private little sneak peeks were all I had left to rely upon. While I started off passing the time innocently intrigued by her rather childlike games of make-believe, I soon found that I had been charmed, hypnotized, wrapped up and carried away by my very own Vivid Imagination—and what's worse, I found her imagery to be strangely resourceful!

Case in point, the fellow who later happened upon my doorstep early one morning brought a sobering hint of validity to these events, which I had naturally assumed were mere figments concocted by Viv, and therefore held no real meaning at all. Considering that by now I had become quite the expert in rustling up a head-full of imaginary friends, it wasn't difficult to discern that this particular fellow would be no figment of my Vivid Imagination. Even so, looking back, I wish he were. At any rate, I did in fact meet his acquaintance, and he did in fact leave with my possessions, a decision I'd later regret. But my oh my, am I getting ahead of myself. There is more, so much more to unfold.

And so Viv continued.

Following a lengthy overnight journey of tending responsibly to Wailing Bellow,

Quiet Breeze, long overdue for a little amusement, blew off the beaten path to frolic among the handful of leaves that had fallen along the roadside below. Wailing Bellow, ill at ease and still harboring remorse concerning his better halves—yet frankly, thankful for a reprieve—was ever so grateful to tag along for the ride.

Quiet Breeze had only just begun to rustle Handful of Leaves, when suddenly she halted as she neared a fork in the road. Straight ahead in the distance, where oddly there was no road at all, she spotted an out-of-the-way antique shop with a hand-painted sign that read THE NOTHING NEW SHOP OF OLD THINGS and she was drawn in that direction.

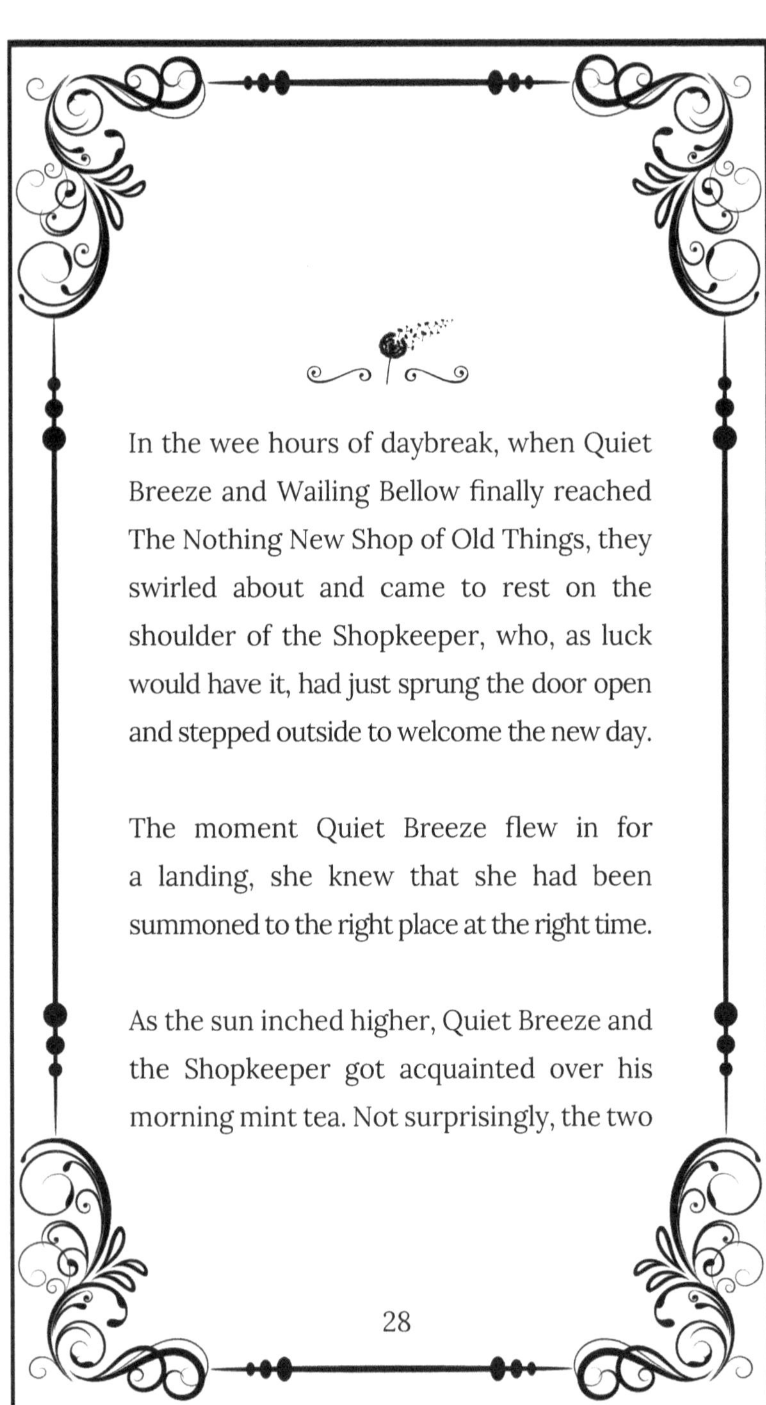

In the wee hours of daybreak, when Quiet Breeze and Wailing Bellow finally reached The Nothing New Shop of Old Things, they swirled about and came to rest on the shoulder of the Shopkeeper, who, as luck would have it, had just sprung the door open and stepped outside to welcome the new day.

The moment Quiet Breeze flew in for a landing, she knew that she had been summoned to the right place at the right time.

As the sun inched higher, Quiet Breeze and the Shopkeeper got acquainted over his morning mint tea. Not surprisingly, the two

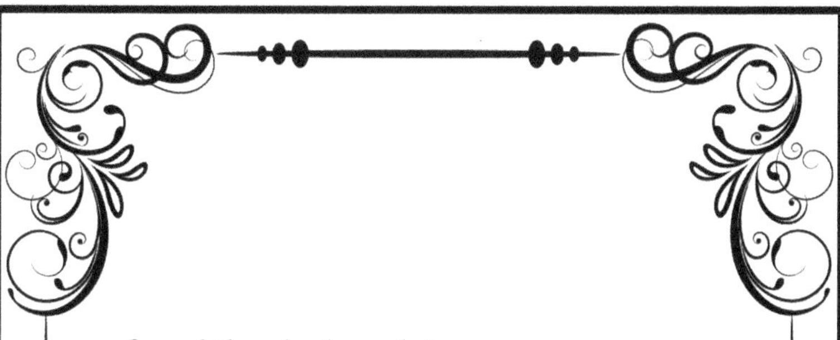

found they had much in common.

"You too?" she inquired.

To which he replied, "Yes, me too!"

The unlikely twosome shared a good-humored laugh, raising their cups and curling their pinkies inward, befitting proper teacup etiquette.

What a delightful affair. Oh, how they carried on!

By now, Quiet Breeze believed Wailing Bellow to be in good hands and readily returned to the fork in the road, where

Handful of Leaves was still patiently awaiting her return. Her rustling of Handful of Leaves to-and-fro, and up and down, and all around caused an infectious flurry of giggles to echo throughout the trees.

Meanwhile, back at The Nothing New Shop of Old Things, Wailing Bellow found himself sipping tea and requesting "two lumps, not three!" while making merry and enjoying the good company and conversation of his would-be rescuer. Wailing Bellow, who, as it turns out, was a bit of a windbag, had all but forgotten about the mission at hand. He was now very nearly all cried out and had quieted down to nothing more than a bothersome snivel in need of a tissue. In fact, things were looking up! Life had just taken a turn for the better, and he hadn't a care in the world. Bothersome Snivel was now perfectly happy, making friends, and making himself at home in the Shopkeeper's eclectic old shop, tucked away just off the beaten path.

With its original stained-glass windows, working radiators, and absence of indoor plumbing, the shop itself was an antique, having been built during the turn of the previous century. The Shopkeeper proudly welcomed Bothersome Snivel to roam freely about his timeless treasure trove that housed a little of this and a lot of that. From the holiday section in the rear, he could hear Bothersome Snivel's *oohs* and *aahs* increasing with every turn, and it pleased the Shopkeeper to know that his guest was content.

The inevitable *ohhhhh* that generally followed such *oohs* and *aahs* came but was unexpectedly cut short and then silenced altogether.

Taken aback, the Shopkeeper immediately rushed toward Bothersome Snivel's silenced *ohhhhh,* discovering it had indeed stopped short and was now curiously suspended in midair above the shop's cozy little library. With his wooden clogs *clip-clopping* down the aisle, the Shopkeeper contemplated the quickest route, then scrambled as fast as his clogged feet could carry him, slowing his gait as he skirted past the menagerie of porcelain figurines displayed in the center of the parlor.

As the Shopkeeper suspected, Bothersome Snivel, mouth still agape, had uncovered the shop's most fascinating work of art, the apple of his eye, the crown jewel, the pièce de résistance! While casually browsing the shop, his sniveling nose had snuffed out the Shopkeeper's prized foreign handkerchief collection and was speechless.

Just out of Bothersome Snivel's reach, a towering glass display case held a beautifully preserved array of imported and priceless monogrammed pocket squares. From Lebanese laced linen, to

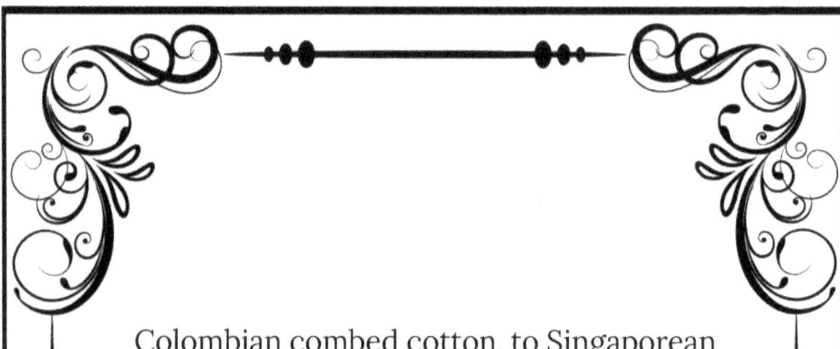

Colombian combed cotton, to Singaporean softened silk, each nameless monogram was hand stitched to perfection.

No longer able to resist, Bothersome Snivel floated right past the Look, But Don't Touch! sign and seeped behind the glass. Just as he rubbed his cheek against the fine fabric, Bothersome Snivel was painfully and regrettably reminded of his own beloved hanky that his dearly departed mudda' used to blot his tears back in the old country when he was but a wee little one. Just then, Bothersome Snivel's stiff upper lip began to quiver. And once more, he was provoked to well up and wail again, each tear bigger, greater, stronger than

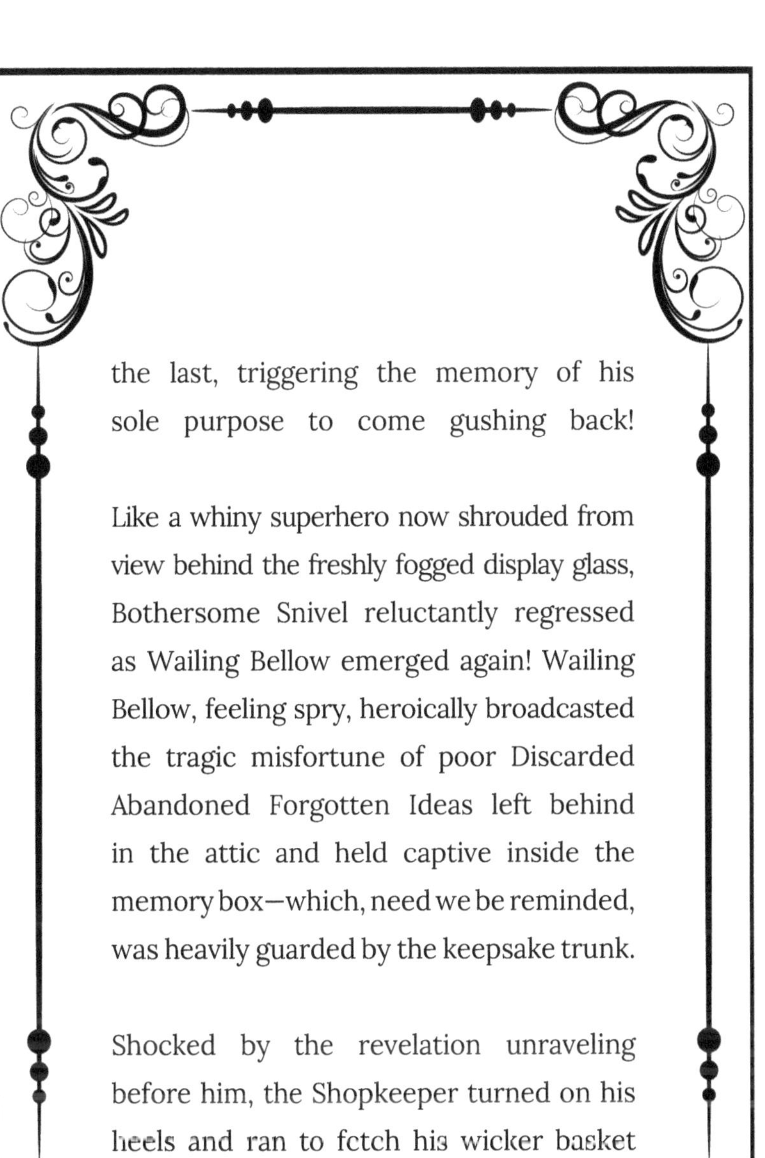

the last, triggering the memory of his sole purpose to come gushing back!

Like a whiny superhero now shrouded from view behind the freshly fogged display glass, Bothersome Snivel reluctantly regressed as Wailing Bellow emerged again! Wailing Bellow, feeling spry, heroically broadcasted the tragic misfortune of poor Discarded Abandoned Forgotten Ideas left behind in the attic and held captive inside the memory box—which, need we be reminded, was heavily guarded by the keepsake trunk.

Shocked by the revelation unraveling before him, the Shopkeeper turned on his heels and ran to fetch his wicker basket and a soft blanket, as he possessed an impeccable knack for, and was often accustomed to caring for these particular cries of the unwanted. He took off toward the front of the shop, shouldering Wailing Bellow as before and again slowing his gait as he skirted past the menagerie of porcelain figurines displayed in the center of the parlor. With Wailing Bellow guiding the way, the peculiar pair headed for the fork in the road, passing through Flurry of Giggles still lingering with Quiet Breeze. They soon disappeared around the bend in hopes that all had not been lost.

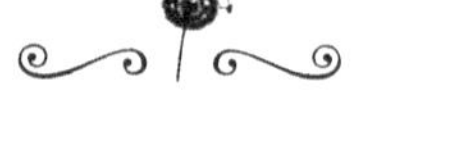

Graciously enduring yet another lengthy journey, this time homeward bound, Wailing Bellow, long overdue for a tissue, drifted off the beaten path to gather a few soft leaves in an effort to blow his stuffy nose. The mighty blow came with such force that his gust of air blasted the peculiar pair right past a charming little WELCOME! sign and straight into town. The Shopkeeper, clogs clinging to his toes, was ever so grateful to tag along for the ride.

At the same time, Vivid Imagination was having the time of her life at my expense. Since early that morning, I had been outside, unusually preoccupied with wielding my rusty watering can like a holy relic and performing resurrections among my parched potted plants, which ordinarily I overlooked and allowed to overrun my back patio. To make matters worse, Viv's latest sneak peek—this time

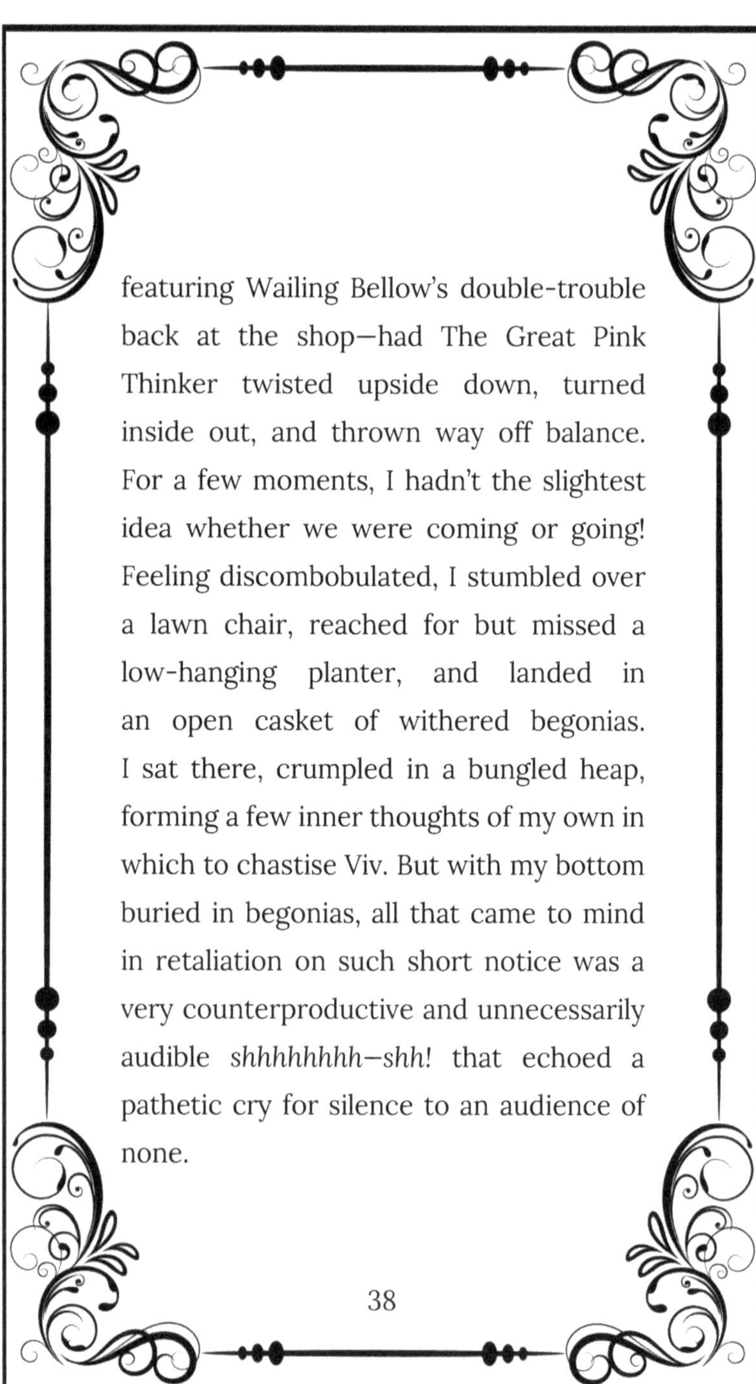

featuring Wailing Bellow's double-trouble back at the shop—had The Great Pink Thinker twisted upside down, turned inside out, and thrown way off balance. For a few moments, I hadn't the slightest idea whether we were coming or going! Feeling discombobulated, I stumbled over a lawn chair, reached for but missed a low-hanging planter, and landed in an open casket of withered begonias. I sat there, crumpled in a bungled heap, forming a few inner thoughts of my own in which to chastise Viv. But with my bottom buried in begonias, all that came to mind in retaliation on such short notice was a very counterproductive and unnecessarily audible *shhhhhhhh—shh!* that echoed a pathetic cry for silence to an audience of none.

But of course, Viv couldn't and wouldn't be silenced. She shot back with a tart inside joke that erupted a not-so-dignified memory of ours up to the surface, baiting me to lash out at her with a shame-on-you finger. The next thing I knew I was mumbling idle threats through pursed lips and clenched teeth. Useless, yet remarkably satisfying.

From over the fence, Old Lady Kirkabee was tending faithfully to her plush autumn blooms of golden sunflowers, orange sneezeweed, amber mums, scarlet zinnias, burgundy roses, black-eyed Susans, purple pansies, and even a variety of deep blue asters sprinkled among the foliage —complete with an assortment of birds and bees and butterflies of course. I believe the only thing missing was a winged unicorn soaring over a rainbow. *My oh my, how I do digress with such envy!*

In any case, Old Lady Kirkabee, my flowered fence-mate, stole a long, concerned look at me, the crazed lunatic practically swinging from the rafters, shushing the shadows, and suddenly watering my graveyard past its redemption. Twiddling her green thumbs and contemplating her next move, the sprightly old gal scooped up her fat cat, Harold, took a few calculated steps backward and made a cautious beeline back into the safety of her own home. *Swish! Boom! Click!* The door slid with a rolling thunder and latched with a quickness.

Moments later, I was answering an unsolicited knock at my front door.

"Good day!" declared the Shopkeeper, whom I thought to be a bit more chipper than one ought to be allowed at that hour of the morning. Promptly, he removed his hat. His kind, wholesome, tender-hearted eyes pierced straight through me, unmoved by my nonchalant expression and lack of enthusiasm toward his greeting.

"*Meh*," said I.

Clearing his throat, the Shopkeeper repeated his salutation as Wailing Bellow ducked behind his collar. "Good day," he persisted, clutching his hat to his chest and channeling a more tolerable tone. "Might you be willing to rid yourself of any old, unwanted things today? Nothing new, mind you," probed the Shopkeeper, as his delicately aged hands held out a small, tattered wicker basket lined with a soft blue blanket for the rescue of Discarded Abandoned Forgotten Ideas.

I tried desperately to ignore the handwritten tag attached to the front of the basket that read HANDLE WITH GREAT CARE. How this fishy fellow came to know I was harboring unwanted things of old, I did not know, nor did I inquire.

Slowly, I eyeballed this fishy fellow from the top of his curly, silver-streaked locks that stood on end in a frenzy and twinned with his brows, right down to those clumsy clogs *clippety-cloppetying* on my front doorstep.

"Hmmm," said I.

Coldly, I stood there. Boldly, he did too.

Just then, a sudden unsettling and rather puzzling wave of déjà vu washed through me, interrupting the awkwardness. For a spell, I was certain we shared a moment of familiarity. I called upon Viv. Shockingly, she offered no comment. *Hmph!* I consulted The Great Pink Thinker, and a vague glimpse of his likeness skirted past. Did I know him? But more importantly, how could I have so easily forgotten such an unforgettable face?

Something in his eyes, those big, deep, marblesque eyes, compelled me to comply.

"Wait right here!" said I.

Elated to finally free myself from the agony in the attic, I sprinted up the stairs, burst into the upper room, broke open the trunk, snatched my memory box, flew back down the stairs, and thrust the box carelessly into the Shopkeeper's basket, bidding him and them a fond fare-thee-well and good riddance!

In turn, the Shopkeeper gently, neatly, safely, and securely set the box right side up, then began to bundle the box with a fold, tuck here and a fold, tuck there overlapping each corner flawlessly as though he had rehearsed it a thousand times. Tightly swaddled in a lamb's wool blanket of periwinkle blue, Discarded Abandoned Forgotten Ideas was about as blessed as a bundled box could be.

All the while, I'd been irritatingly curious about the little apparition hiding behind the Shopkeeper's collar, moaning a solo identical to the agony I'd just evicted from my attic. And so, seeing my glare fixed on the Shopkeeper still loitering at my front door, Wailing Bellow shuddered and shrunk to the size of a whisper. Suddenly, being caged deep within my memory box again didn't seem so bad after all. Leaving behind a pint-sized puddle of tears on the Shopkeeper's lapel, Whisper took one huge plunge forward into the basket, eased

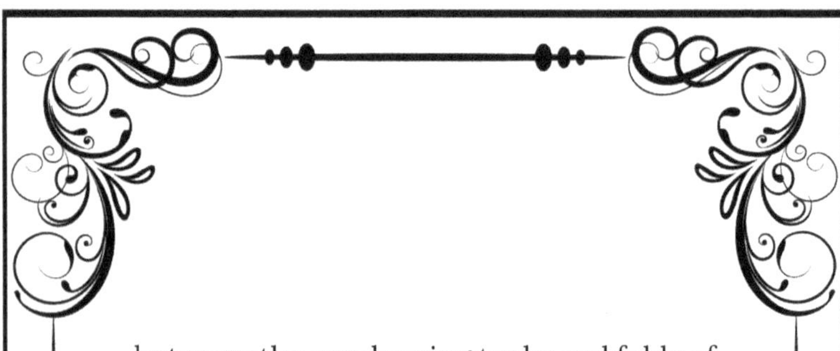

between the overlapping tucks and folds of the lamb's wool blanket, and escaped back into the box, practically unnoticed.

What a peculiar pair, thought I.

And with that, the Shopkeeper thanked me, tipped his hat with a gracious smile, and made his leave. In the span of sixty seconds flat, I had wiped my hands clean of the entire ordeal. Then, with a sigh of awkward relief, coupled with a double dose of wavering satisfaction, again I withdrew to my well-worn, sensible sitting chair, and like a rookie empty-nester, kicked up my feet.

Where I sat.
And sat.
And sat some more.

Because, after all, it was just an Idea.

Wasn't it?

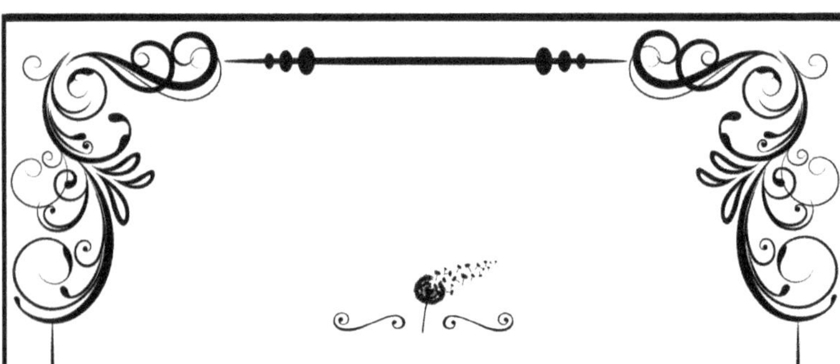

The Shopkeeper wasted no time on the road returning to The Nothing New Shop of Old Things. Every few steps or so, his clogged feet would skip a step or two, and then three, and then four, briefly defying gravity and pausing only momentarily to check the well-being of the blue bundle in the basket.

As he approached his shop, he dashed through the front entrance, once again remembering to slow his gait as he skirted past the menagerie of porcelain figurines displayed in the center of the parlor. Regaining his speed, he darted out of the rear exit, where he finally came to a full stop in the courtyard.

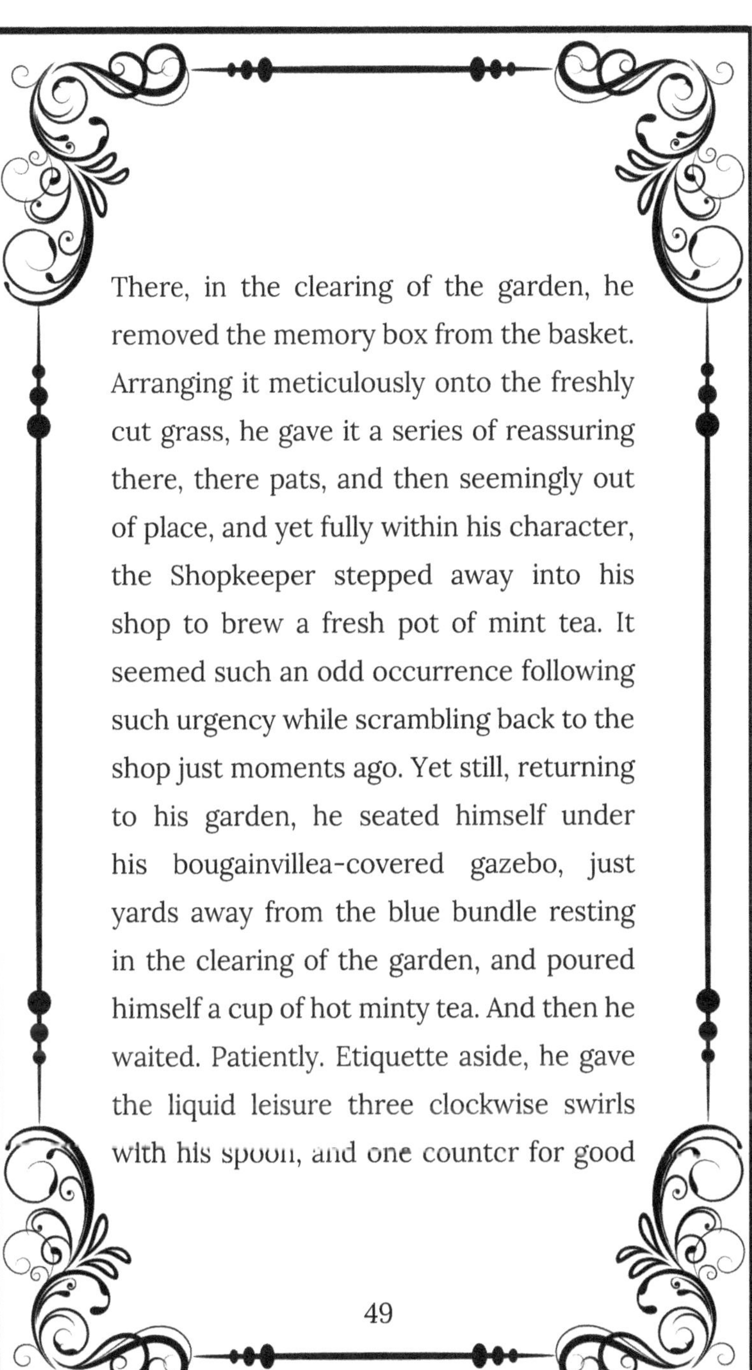

There, in the clearing of the garden, he removed the memory box from the basket. Arranging it meticulously onto the freshly cut grass, he gave it a series of reassuring there, there pats, and then seemingly out of place, and yet fully within his character, the Shopkeeper stepped away into his shop to brew a fresh pot of mint tea. It seemed such an odd occurrence following such urgency while scrambling back to the shop just moments ago. Yet still, returning to his garden, he seated himself under his bougainvillea-covered gazebo, just yards away from the blue bundle resting in the clearing of the garden, and poured himself a cup of hot minty tea. And then he waited. Patiently. Etiquette aside, he gave the liquid leisure three clockwise swirls with his spoon, and one counter for good

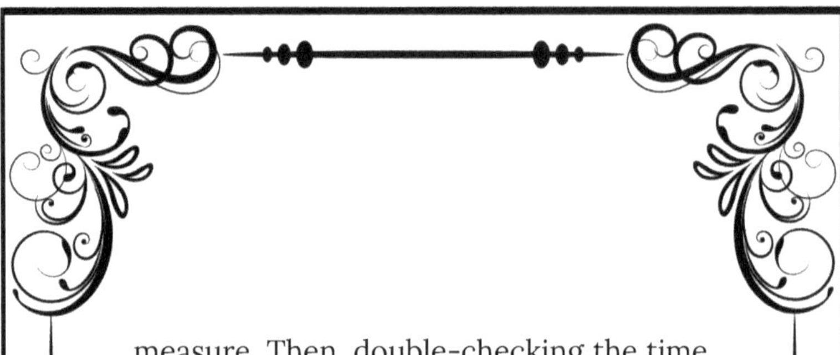

measure. Then, double-checking the time, he glanced down at his pocket watch, and again, he waited. This time, twice as long and twice as patient.

Vivid Imagination displayed this to me so vividly that I could have sworn I was right there in the garden within an arm's reach of the Shopkeeper. By the power of her suggestion, a waft of sweet mint filled my nostrils. Hot steam warmed the tip of my nose and fogged my eyeglasses. At any moment I fully expected to hear the Shopkeeper's voice declare "Come out, come out wherever you are," nudging me to come forth from behind the gazebo, bougainvillea Velcroed throughout my

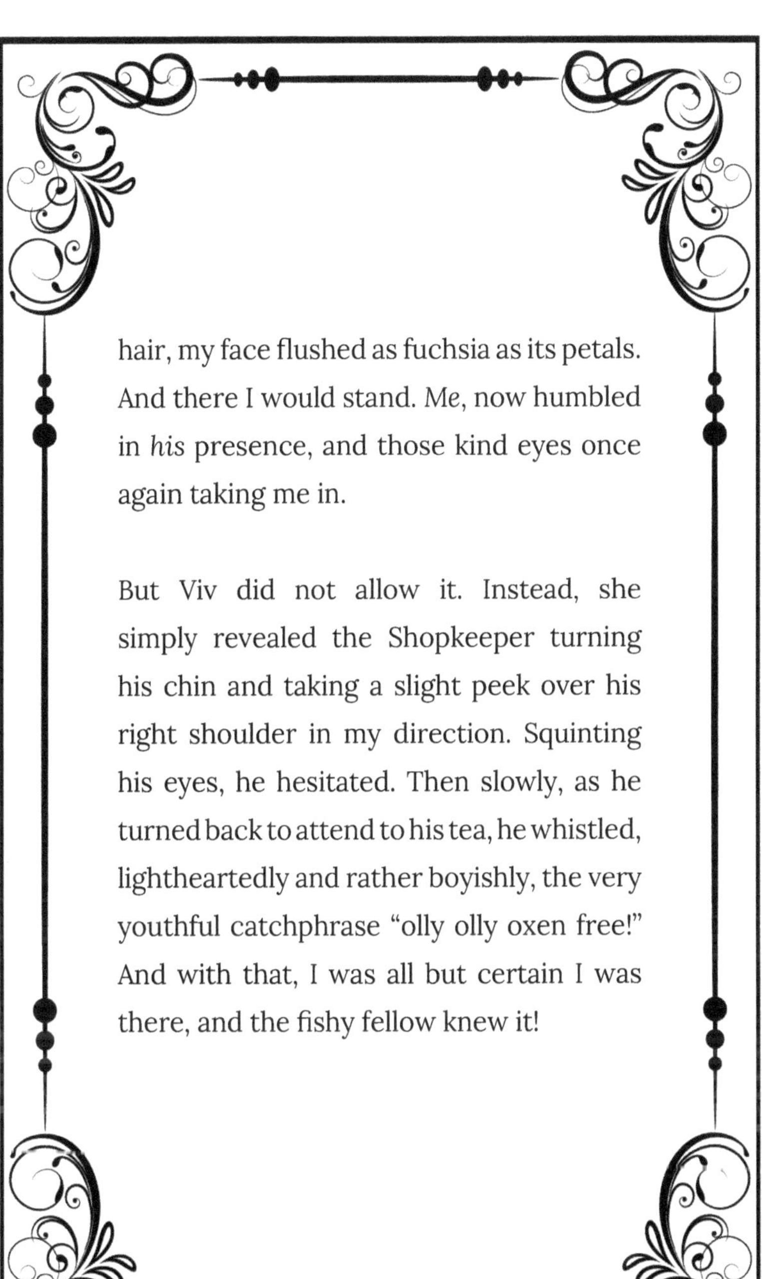

hair, my face flushed as fuchsia as its petals. And there I would stand. *Me*, now humbled in *his* presence, and those kind eyes once again taking me in.

But Viv did not allow it. Instead, she simply revealed the Shopkeeper turning his chin and taking a slight peek over his right shoulder in my direction. Squinting his eyes, he hesitated. Then slowly, as he turned back to attend to his tea, he whistled, lightheartedly and rather boyishly, the very youthful catchphrase "olly olly oxen free!" And with that, I was all but certain I was there, and the fishy fellow knew it!

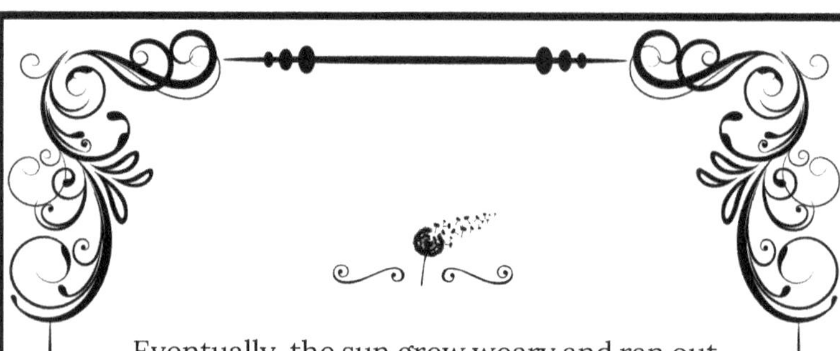

Eventually, the sun grew weary and ran out of patience, and despite its best efforts, laid down and dozed off behind the dusk, giving way to the moon to take precedence in the night sky. In his waiting, the Shopkeeper linked one leg over the other, dangling one clog above its mate to fend for itself. Casually, as though all was well with the world, he grabbed his favorite deck of cards and settled in for a long game of Forty Thieves.

Now *this* was preposterous! It was one thing to brew and then enjoy a cup of hot tea, but to busy himself with a trivial game of solitaire was something else altogether different. Again, taking such pause after such urgency stumped me. What was he up to? I couldn't make heads or tails of it. I decided his sanity was questionable at best. Was he mad? Was he delusional? Had he taken temporary leave of his senses? Though I wanted desperately to hear the answers to these questions and more, suddenly he shuffled the deck, and my ears fell prey instead to the soothing sound of the shuffle's unwavering velvet ripple and the soft, slippery snap of the cards as they surrendered their rigid ways one by one to the trusted fingers of the Shopkeeper. Each card was selectively recruited, then scrutinized, and finally appointed in sequence to its own proper place. I watched in awe, intrigued at how easily they gave up and gave in, lying down so

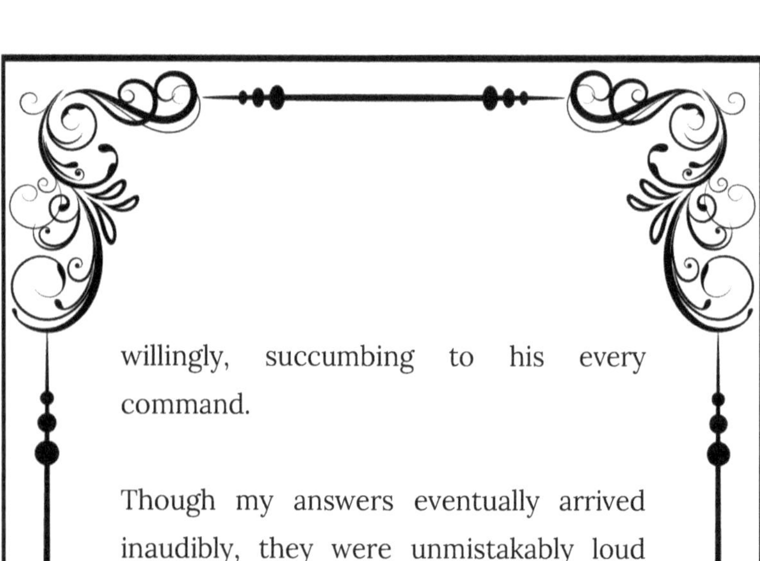

willingly, succumbing to his every command.

Though my answers eventually arrived inaudibly, they were unmistakably loud and clear. In fact, there was now no question that the Shopkeeper was indeed perfectly sane. And so, being of sound mind and body, he performed these tasks with intention and purpose. For the Shopkeeper understood what most did not. That is, that Timing. Is. Everything. And that both good and extraordinary opportunities come to those who not only wait, but to those who tarry expectantly and occupy the in-between time joyfully, managing to find themselves in the right places at the right times.

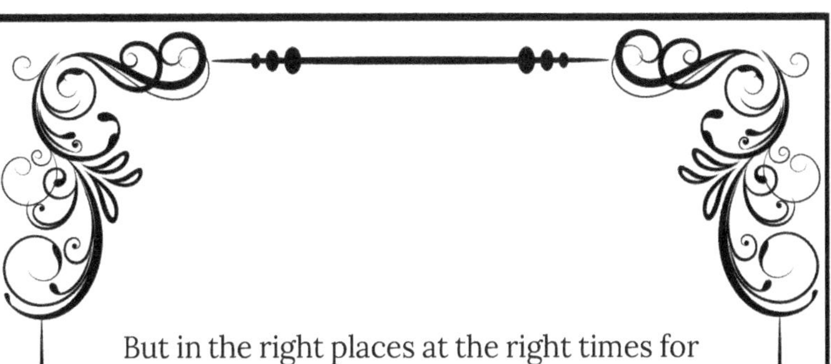

But in the right places at the right times for what purpose?

The Shopkeeper, stirred by the notion that timing is everything, glanced down at his pocket watch once more, and out of the blue the much-anticipated signal he had been waiting for came. Just like that. No pomp. No circumstance. Just a small, unassuming, somewhat inconspicuous ringing sound of a little boy's brass bicycle bell trrringing in the distance, swiftly followed by an obscure thwack. Small, yet quite pivotal in the scheme of things. The Shopkeeper, as though lightening had struck him, promptly jumped to his feet and scrambled as fast as his clogs could carry him just a few yards away, where the

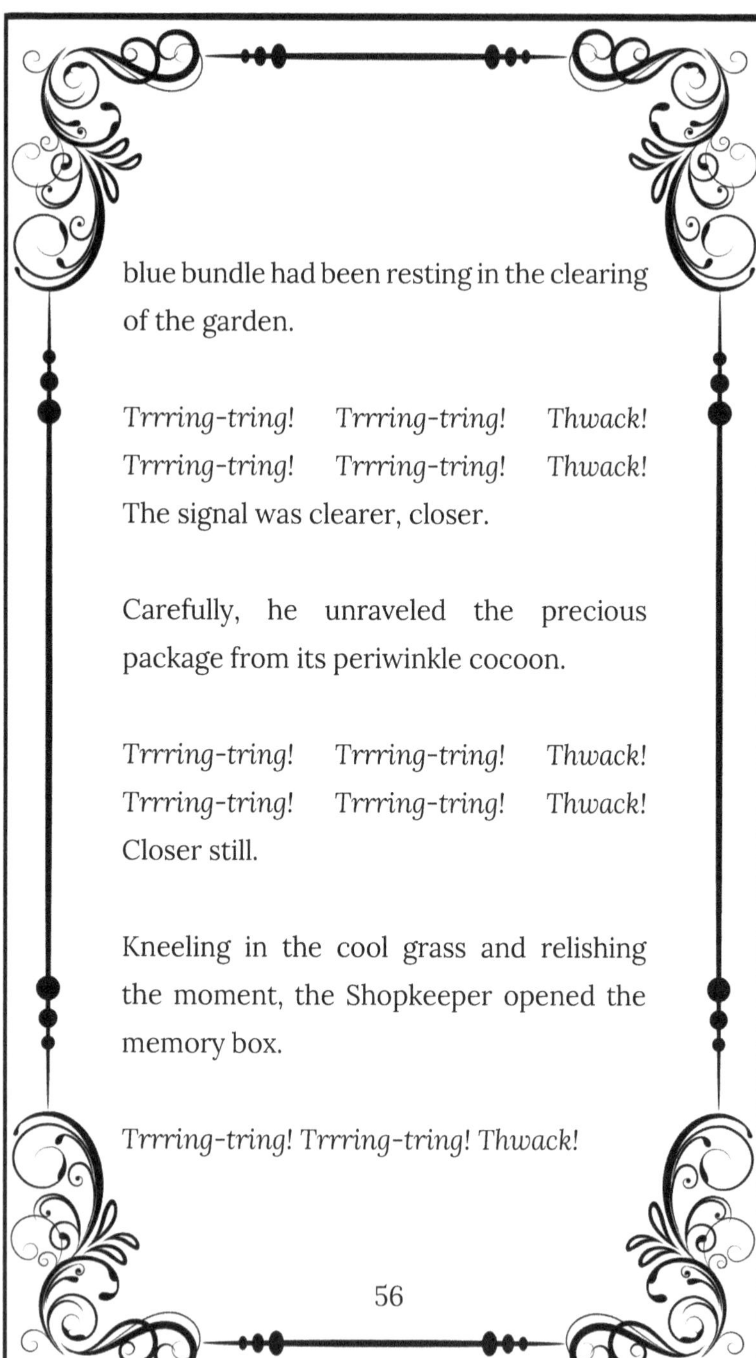

blue bundle had been resting in the clearing of the garden.

Trrring-tring! Trrring-tring! Thwack!
Trrring-tring! Trrring-tring! Thwack!
The signal was clearer, closer.

Carefully, he unraveled the precious package from its periwinkle cocoon.

Trrring-tring! Trrring-tring! Thwack!
Trrring-tring! Trrring-tring! Thwack!
Closer still.

Kneeling in the cool grass and relishing the moment, the Shopkeeper opened the memory box.

Trrring-tring! Trrring-tring! Thwack!

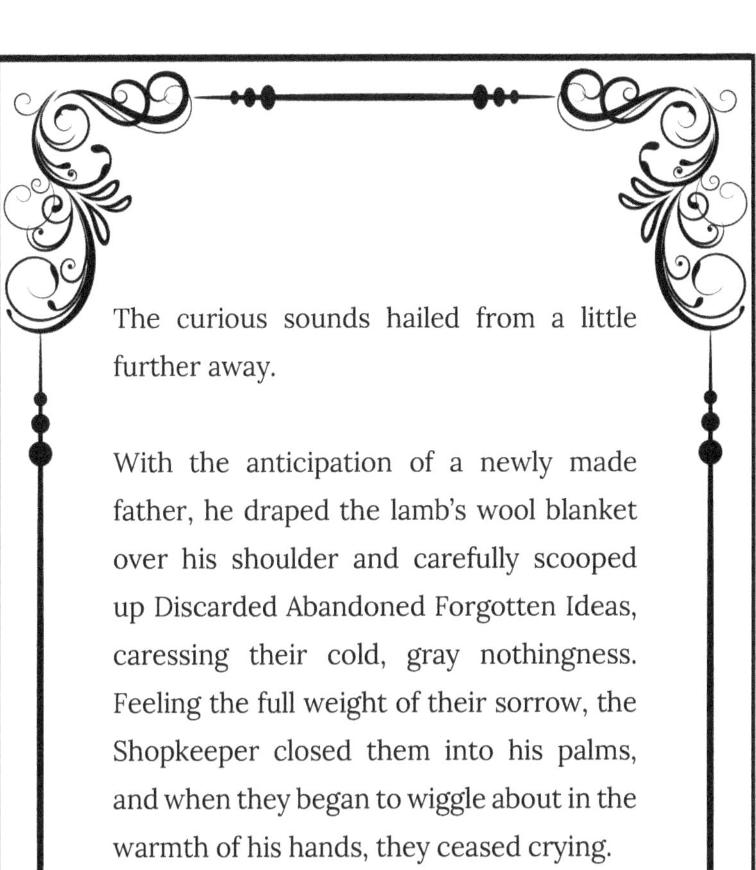

The curious sounds hailed from a little further away.

With the anticipation of a newly made father, he draped the lamb's wool blanket over his shoulder and carefully scooped up Discarded Abandoned Forgotten Ideas, caressing their cold, gray nothingness. Feeling the full weight of their sorrow, the Shopkeeper closed them into his palms, and when they began to wiggle about in the warmth of his hands, they ceased crying.

No longer essential, Wailing Bellow dug himself free from the bottom of the nothingness and rose eye to eye with the Shopkeeper. The two friends shared a split second of silence. With a courageous facade,

Wailing Bellow mustered up a cheerful smile. But his heart strings tugged at his stiff upper lip till he could no longer choke back the telltale signs of sibling rivalry between sorrow and joy, now squabbling for his attention. Helping himself to the lamb's wool blanket from the Shopkeeper's shoulder, the tears fell, and Wailing Bellow blew his nose one last time. Then, just as suddenly as his arrival in the attic, all at once and without warning, Wailing Bellow and the coveted blue blanket evaporated into thin air.

Trrring-tring! Trrring-tring! Thwack! The long-awaited signal was now growing more and more distant.

It was now or never.

The Shopkeeper lifted Discarded Abandoned Forgotten Ideas to his lips, and with a still, small voice, he declared these words of affirmation:

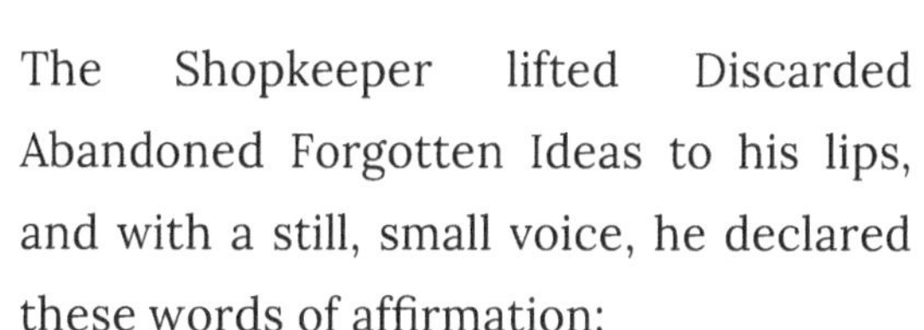

A BRIGHT IDEA
YOU CANNOT SMOTHER.

ITS GIFT IS PROMISED
TO ANOTHER!

Then, he drew in one long, deep breath. Finally, with a single puff, he blew them back into existence.

Like cottony fluffs of a dandelion, Discarded Abandoned Forgotten Ideas whirled high, high into the sky, their radiant glow rcigniting. Each bloom became a light in the darkness as it drifted away toward the horizon, seeking whom it may inspire.

However, Idea, my brightest, most glorious, spectacular, magnificent, extraordinarily fantastical idea, was swept up, up, and away in a breath of fresh air, where he continually whispered his secrets into the open. Until one keen, bright-eyed, gutsy go-getter, who had just stepped outside to grab the evening newspaper, caught wind of it.

Trrring-tring! Trrring-tring! went the paperboy's brass bicycle bell. Right on schedule, as he pedaled faithfully down the street on his usual route. *Thwack!* went the newspaper as it smacked hard against its intended target, third step up from the bottom. Bingo! Spot on!

"Thanks, kiddo!" shouted Gutsy Go-Getter, whose tone was a bit more chipper than one ought to be allowed when simply greeting the paperboy. But on this night, Gutsy had sensed something special, something restless in the air, and thus tarried outside on his front porch a little longer than usual. Suddenly longing for a full whiff of the cool, crisp air, Gutsy inhaled one long, deep breath. Then out of nowhere, eyes wide and index finger jabbing into the air, he exhaled the words "I've got an Idea!"

Operation Dandelion: Complete.

The well-timed opportunity was worth the wait. The deed was done, and the *trrring-tring! trrring-tring! thwacks!* grew faint again as the paperboy pedaled on down the block.

As it turned out, Gutsy Go-Getter was quite the industrious pioneer, and so, naturally, he was just curious enough, just bold enough, just downright plucky enough to breathe intention and purpose back into Idea so that he lived again and took on a whole new life of his own.

The following year, Idea made the front page of every major newspaper across the four corners of the world. One fine summer morning, my radio blasted Idea's success throughout my entire living room.

"Breaking news! This just in! The World's Brand Spanking New and Improved Glorious, Spectacular, Magnificent, Extraordinarily Fantastical Idea will be strolling through his hometown today during the mayor's parade, led by none other than Mayor Jones's Jubilee Band! Beginning at noon sharp! Remember, today only! Don't miss it, and don't delay!"

I leaped from my sitting chair and scurried about for a bit in awe and disbelief. Had Idea returned to me? I gathered my senses and made my way into town.

As I approached Main Street, my heart began to race. Throngs of fans lined the streets, and the boisterous sounds of the Mayor's Jubilee Band led me to a plush red carpet that paved the way to a familiar glow that I couldn't quite make out from the outskirts of the crowd. So I pressed and plowed through to the front of the mob to get a closer look. And there, in the midst of the paparazzi and a cloud of brilliant flashes, stood Idea, displayed on a golden pedestal.

Once again, Idea and I were face-to-face. We locked eyes. By sheer instinct, I reached out to take hold of Idea. But he drew back, tilted his head, and gave me a rather inquisitive look. It was then that I realized Idea had no memory of me. In the span of a few seasons, I had been wiped clean from his history. Saddened, my hands dropped to my sides. And with that, the new owners, Gutsy & Co., thrust Idea up onto their strong, broad shoulders and paraded my Idea through town as their own. The bustling herd of mesmerized onlookers followed in hot pursuit.

"Hip, hip hooray!" they shouted. "Hip, hip hooray for Gutsy's Go-Go-Gizmo!"

What a name they had chosen for my Idea.

Now, standing all alone, I felt empty. The crowd and its clatter of unbridled fanfare had moved on. In its place arose a profound hindsight of Viv and her former hi-jinks. I was reminded of how she'd previously toyed with my sensibilities until my hysteria had run its course. In particular, her obnoxiously vivid sneak peek that played out on my back patio came to mind. Those few moments during my glimpse into Wailing Bellow's forgotten grand mission and the mystery of my discombobulation that ultimately landed me crumpled in a bungled heap with my bottom buried in begonias came rushing back.

In the grand scheme of things, I realized that all of Viv's mischief, her antics, her wayward wisdom was not in vain. It was only then, in the deafening quiet of that moment, that the veil was finally lifted, and all doubt was removed that this same still, small voice of the Shopkeeper, some time ago and unbeknownst to me, had spent its fair share making rounds to The Great Pink Thinker. To me, me! An unlikely Jane Doe, a small fry, a long shot . . . a nobody. *I* had been chosen to participate in an extraordinary opportunity. *I* had been entrusted with a gift to which my initial reply was a somber and indifferent *meh*, then ultimately an emphatic and resounding *no*! Thus, the fishy fellow, the keeper of The Nothing New Shop of Old Things, had been self-appointed to right the wrong.

Slowly, I shuffled back home and slumped back down into my same ole, well-worn, sensible sitting chair.

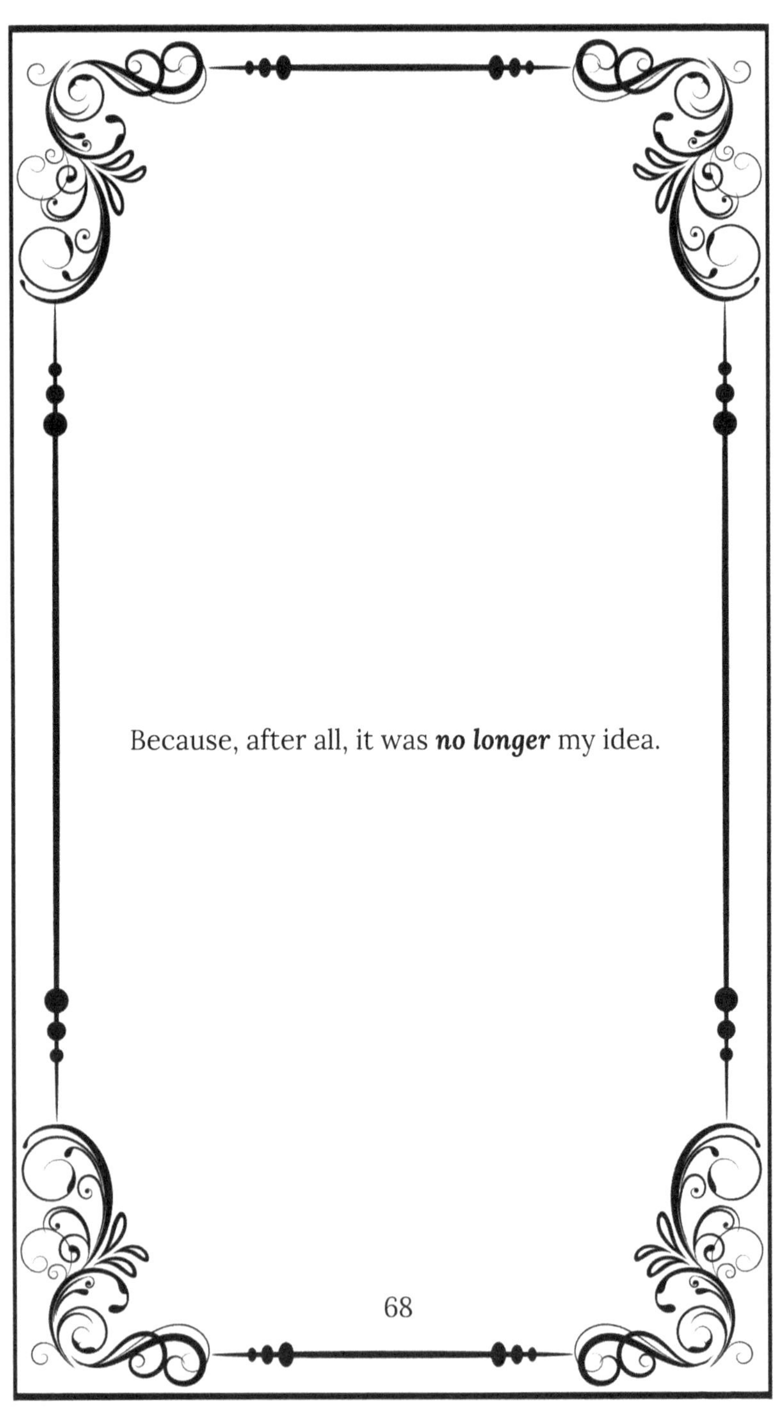

Because, after all, it was **no longer** my idea.

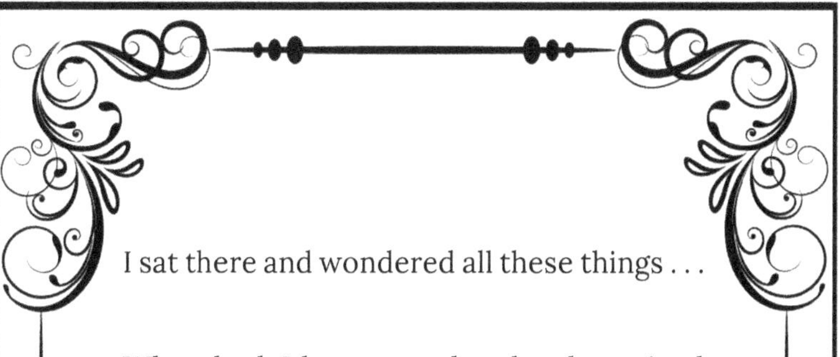

I sat there and wondered all these things . . .

What had Idea seen the day he raised an eyebrow and gazed afar off into our future? Which doors might have been opened to me had I taken Idea's advice and strolled uptown to rub elbows with the Big Enchiladas? What tales could I have told? What works could I have written had I not plucked Idea from his throne and banished him to a shelf among the riffraff?

As expected, the sun grew weary and dozed off yet again, giving way to the moon to take precedence in the night sky. Surprisingly, when the sun awakened, it found that I was still sitting and still wondering. Exactly how *did* that fishy fellow happen upon my doorstep—that stranger whose impeccable timing couldn't have been more perfect? All I could muster up to do was just sit there and marvel at the wonder of how Gutsy & Co. caught wind of an Idea I'd forgotten long ago.

With great effort, I peeled myself from my well-worn, sensible sitting chair and schlepped to the kitchen to brew myself a pot of hot coffee. Steadying my pour, I filled my cup to the brim, all the while wondering at what point had it been decided that my Idea be handed over to another.

I sat there, on the edge of my seat, face cradled in my palms, wondering how many nations around the globe may have benefited sooner had I introduced Idea to the four corners of the world several seasons prior.

Sadly, I sat there and couldn't help but wonder how much more laughter could have been heard from rambunctious children romping around the house with Idea had I not busied myself with affairs that required less effort, but ultimately brought less joy.

Finally, I stood up and I wondered how best to kick myself for neglecting to cash in on the most valuable two cents I'd gleaned from *Your Big Idea* and *How Not to Screw It Up!*

I sat back down, and I wondered all these things, until . . .

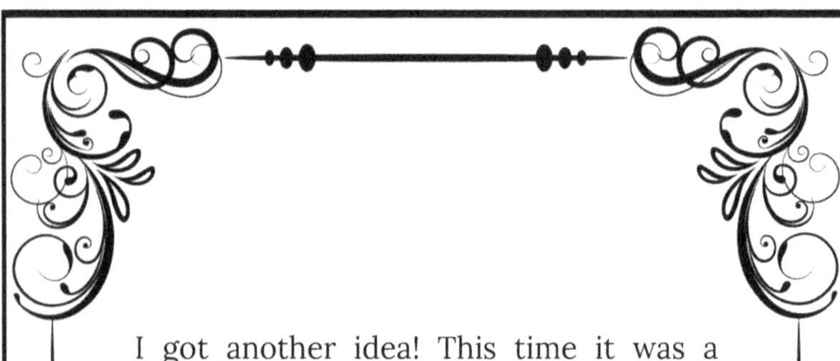

I got another idea! This time it was a marvelous, stupendous, incredibly remarkable, delightfully ingenious idea!

Eagerly, so's not to forget, I grabbed a pencil and scratched it out, in its entirety, on an old, coffee-stained notepad I'd dug out from among a stack of outdated magazines, junk mail, overdue bills, and the like that had obviously in a pinch once doubled as a trivet.

Then just as before, I headed toward . . . the shelf.

Only this time, I reached for my old trusty typewriter!

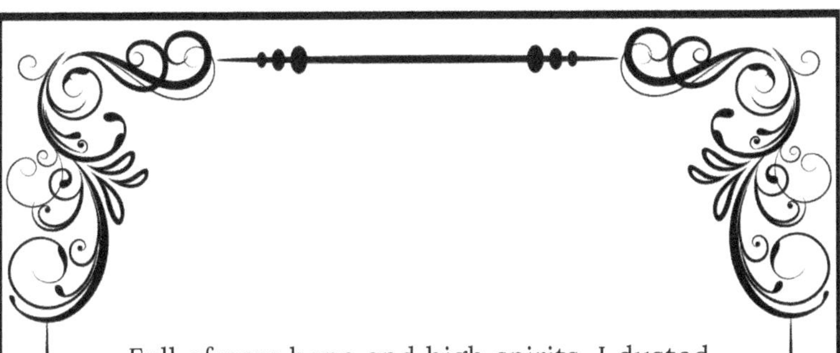

Full of new hope and high spirits, I dusted each key thoroughly, pulled my shoulders back, and propped myself up into my *thinking* chair.

Where I typed.
And typed.
And typed some more,

permitting Inner Child to run tirelessly, deep within the walls of The Great Pink Thinker until Viv unfolded the marvelous, stupendous, incredibly remarkable, delightfully ingenious tale you've just read.

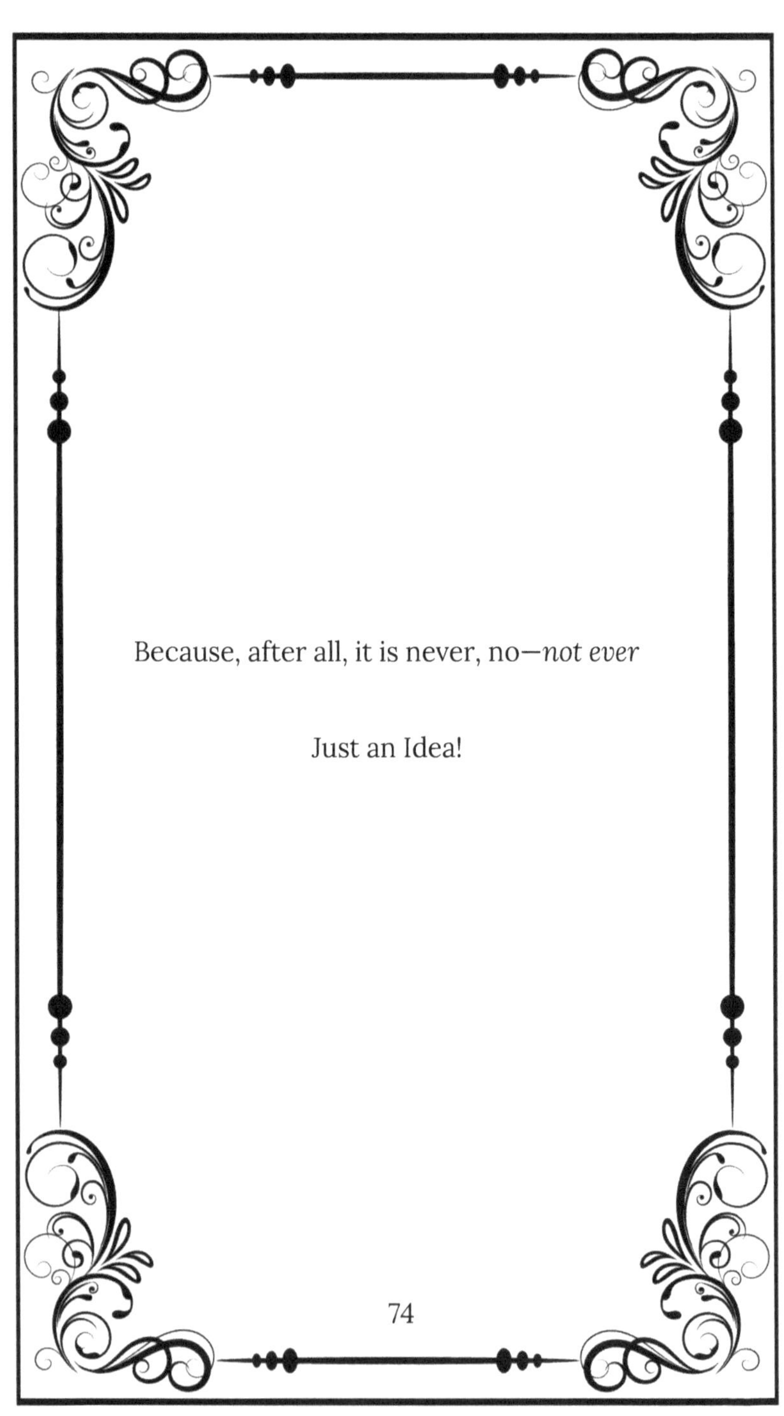

Because, after all, it is never, no—*not ever*

Just an Idea!

THE END